The Six Bells of Ruskington Village

From a selection of stories written by the
**pupils of Winchelsea and Chestnut Street
primary schools**, Ruskington, Lincolnshire.
Chosen by the children's author, Joyce Dunbar.

Illustrations by Russell Turner.

ISBN: Softcover   978-1-9845-9012-1
         Hardcover   978-1-9845-9013-8
         EBook   978-1-9845-9011-4

Photographs of the interior and exterior of All Saints' church,
Ruskington are reproduced by kind permission of Julian P
Guffogg

Print information available on the last page

Rev. date: 07/03/2019

To order additional copies of this book, contact:
Xlibris
0800-056-3182
www.xlibrispublishing.co.uk
Orders@ Xlibrispublishing.co.uk

The Six Bells of Ruskington Village

Some of the adventures of Bessie, Belle, Boo, Billy
(and his pet bat, Belfry), Bob, and Benny

From an original idea by Debra Wadsley

In support of the Ruskington Bells Restoration Fund

I ♥ **Ruskington**
With bells on

Thanks!

This wonderful collection of stories has been some time in the making. That's because of all the hard work of lots of people. Here is a big Thank You!! to the individuals who helped out the most to make this published book happen:

The children and teachers at Winchelsea and Chestnut Street primary schools who wrote and painted for the love of the bells

Joyce Dunbar – published children's author, originally from Lincolnshire, and our special judge for the final collection of the best twenty stories written by the children

Russell Turner – advocate of story-telling and superb illustrator (from Oxfordshire, but never mind!)

Members of the Ruskington Bells Restoration Fund campaign: that's, Diana Scott Cross, Debra Wadsley, Renata Loj, Alan Dowell, Stephanie Parker and Stephen Wildgoose.

How the Six Bells stories came about

Bessie Bell was feeling her age. After all, she'd been chiming out in a stately fashion for over 400 years. Bob Bell wasn't much younger, and his joints were getting rather stiff.

Belle, Boo, Benny, and Billy (not forgetting Belfry, Billy's pet bat) were spring chickens by comparison, but still way past their 100th birthdays. Even so, Boo was still a little shy of giving out her full ringing tone; Belle was only concerned about the day she would be shiny and beautiful once more; Benny didn't want to be teased any more about his shape; and Billy, well Billy was Billy, and just wanted to play and play.

So, the grown-ups in Ruskington thought they would raise some money to help the bells, and keep them happy, safe and in full, glorious sound for hundreds of years to come.

The children at the Winchelsea and Chestnut Street primary schools fell in love with the bell characters – Bessie, Bob, Boo, Belle, Benny, Billy (and even Belfry!) – and off they went to come up with some fantastic tales about the six bells of Ruskington village.

We all hope you enjoy reading their stories.

Introducing the Six Bells of Ruskington Village

Bessie

- Stately and regal
- Thinks she's Queen Elizabeth I
- Loves dancing
- Hates bad smells

Belle

- Vain, only wants to be beautiful
- None of the bells are shiney enough for her to see her reflection
- Wants to be famous

Belle

- Very shy
- Youngest bell
- Doesnt like to ring because 'people will hear me'

Billy

- Very naughty and cheeky
- Has a pet bat called Belfry
- Likes ringing 'like the clappers'

Bob

- Oldest and wisest
- Doesn't like change
- Lives in the past
- Teller of stories and historical facts

Benny

- Teased because he is tubby - 'Big Benny'
- Gets sad
- Secretly in love with Boo

Contents

When Bob was stolen by robbers

By Lennon

IT WAS A TYPICAL DAY IN RUSKINGTON CHURCH. The sun was shining; all the bells were ringing away to the beat of the music. Away in the corner, Benny was peeking at Boo, as he had a huge crush on her. Belfry, Billy's pet bat, was flying in the sky, flapping his wings as smoothly as the wind blows against your face. It was tea-time and all the bells were ringing out for the villagers to eat.

Night descended. Two robbers approached quietly in a black van. Everyone was asleep. The robbers had a massive bag for one of the bells. They targeted Bob, as he was the oldest and wisest of the six bells – also the most valuable of them all. As they loaded Bob into the van, he woke up so he tried his hardest to escape from the van, but the doors were too strong. After a while, Bob sat down wondering what to do. Suddenly the van stopped. The back doors flew open, but Bob was too tired to try and run away from the van. Right in front of a big, run-down house, the robbers stood in front of the van cheering because they had captured Bob.

Bob shouted, "Help!"

The robbers said, "Shut up and stop shouting – we're all getting bored."

The next day, the bells woke up and they noticed that Bob was missing and everyone was very worried about where he could be. But the bells noticed tyre tracks on the road. All five bells went looking for him.

All night the bells followed the tyre tracks until they arrived at a place where the tracks suddenly stopped short. In front of them now they could see the grooves in the dirt from where they had dragged Bob along the ground. The building was very disgusting and horrible. They went inside the place. It was like a maze and all the bells got lost in different sections of that horrible house. Billy entered one room, looked inside into the gloom and spotted Bob tied up with chains. Then suddenly, Billy heard some men coming towards him, so he went and hid under a table.

The two robbers walked into the room and noticed that the chains were nearly untied. Bob started to shift about loosening the chains further, hoping they would fall off. And they did. Billy snuck up behind the two robbers and clapped their heads together so that they fell to the ground, unconscious. But the doors were locked. Billy had an idea to search the robber's pockets for the keys, but he couldn't find any. Bob saw the keys down the corridor and guessed that they keys had fallen out when the robbers were walking down to check on Bob. Billy noticed that the window was open, so they both shouted outside, "HELP!!" to see if anyone could hear.

Benny did hear, and ran up the stairs, looking for the keys. Where were they? Eventually, he found the bunch of keys, and soon got the right one to unlock the door. Quickly, Billy and Bob ran outside to the others, with great relief.

Later on, all six bells rang 999 for the police to come and arrest the robbers right away. Then Bob, Billy, Bessie, Benny, Boo, and Belle went out for a lovely meal together to celebrate the rescue of Bob – and the capture of the two robbers.

Night descended and all six bells walked home, holding each other's hand. They came up to the church, climbed the bell tower and fell asleep all at the same time as they were so tired from rescuing Bob. The robbers served a miserable life in prison for the rest of their lives, as the police were looking for them anyway for stealing lots of valuable things from many people. And, of course, Belfry was very happy to be with Billy again.

When Belle and Bessie met a lion - and the bell tower got a clean!

By Tilly

IN THE EXTREMELY UNTIDY BELL TOWER OF RUSKINGTON ALL SAINTS CHURCH, six rusty old bells danced gracefully in the cold, delicate breeze from the smashed window. The bells names are: Belle, who wants to be famous; Boo, who is very shy; Bessie, who thinks she is the queen; Billy, who is always naughty, Bob, who is extremely old; and, Benny, who is teased for being chubby.

In the bell tower, you could see: smashed glass from the broken window, millions of live spiders, dead spiders, rats, mice, broken bricks and, of course, the bells. Tonight, Bob is telling a fascinating story about the last time he was inspected; whilst Belle and Bessie are doing each other's make-up for their club on how to get famous. This is a normal Friday evening.

Then Belle and Bessie set off, so they wouldn't be late for the club. They have to go underground to get there …. when unexpectedly, a stranger grabbed them and threw them in the dark, terrifying, soulless forest – for no reason.

They were terrified. In the morning, the other bells were worried sick about Belle and Bessie, so they jumped out of the window and started off in different directions. Boo went north – in the direction of Belle and Bessie as it turned out. Bob went south, Billy went east, and Benny went west. Later that day, Boo got a glimpse of Bessie and Belle in the horrible forest being circled by a lion. Boo was really, really scared, but she knew she had to be brave and rescue them.

First, she distracted the lion by shouting as loud as possible: "LION, LEAVE MY FRIENDS ALONE!". The lion was terrified at the noise and ran off. Since Bessie and Belle were frozen with fear, Boo had to carry them back. But before they could go home, Boo, Belle and Bessie had to go and find the other bells. That done, Boo didn't have to carry Belle and Bessie anymore, which made Boo sigh in relief. When they returned home, they decided after hundreds of years living there to clean it up. Out went: the mice, rats, flies, bats and the cobwebs, straight out of the window and they fell on the passing people!

Now Belle and Bessie have replaced Boo as being VERY shy and Boo is extremely brave, and that's the new now.

When teamwork saved Billy from the top of the tower

By Sophie

IT WAS A WARM SUMMER'S DAY. Vibrantly coloured birds were chirping and the sky was light blue. Everyone was doing their normal thing.

Belle was gazing in a shiny mirror; Bessie was gracefully parading around the bell tower; Boo was asleep; Bob was telling Benny about his past adventures; and Billy was playing tig with Belfry (that's Billy's naughty pet bat).

Belfry was 'It', so Billy ran away and climbed up the tower of Ruskington All Saints Church to silently hide right up at the top. However, Billy didn't know that Belfry was up there too to get a better view. Belfry tapped Billy, and he let out one massive scream:

"OWW HELP!!", Billy screamed.

As the night sky descended and everything turned cold, Belfry quickly zoomed inside exhausted from trying to pull Billy up and he got Bob to help out. Bob immediately said yes and ran outside. He tried, and tried but couldn't get Billy up. Then he decided to get everyone else to help. It took quite a while to convince Bessie and Belle because they didn't want to get themselves wet or dirty and because they had a very important party to go to, but eventually they said yes (although they did warn everyone that if they broke a nail, they wouldn't ring ever again).

We need a plan !!!

Sprinting as fast as everyone could (except for Bessie and Belle, who were dawdling), they raced over to check if Billy was in pain. And he was. Billy was in lots of pain. So, everyone held hands to make a chain; Billy tried to put up his hand but it only moved a bit – but that was good enough. Then suddenly, there was another scream:

"AHHH!"

Belle had got herself muddy. But she kept trying and that gave her more confidence and she hooked her foot over the pile of dirt so Boo could grab Billy a bit more. But then Belle slipped and everyone was stuck in the filthy hole on top of Billy. "We need a plan," said Bob.

First, they picked Billy up so they could have a think, including Billy and Belfry. Finally, Benny found a way out:

"What if we do exactly the same thing as before and pull each other up?" he said wisely.

Everyone liked that idea and they pulled each other up with one huge push, and then everyone was free.

After that, Belle learnt that being shiny and clean wasn't the most important thing in the world. Billy was less cheeky but Belfry decided to stay as naughty as ever. Benny was still tubby but he was now one of the strongest and bravest – because he likes to do things no-one else can.

When Boo made a big impression

By Beth and Aimee

"BILLY! GET THAT BAT OFF ME. He's getting muddy prints all over my glorious bell!" screeched Belle. With her bell not being quite so shiny anymore, Billy, who was trying to get his hat down, was laughing out loud.

"OK, OK Belle, calm down. The bell-ringer is due to come up because it's almost 12:00pm, so he will clean you then," sighed Bob, who was TRYING to get some rest.

Ding Dong Ding Dong!

"POST!" they all screamed! Suddenly men and the bell-ringer came up carrying a big box and some ladders from the council. The bell-ringer gave a sly smile to the others then he walked off downstairs. Sitting next to Bessie was Boo, a small, shiny bell, who had a lilac bow attached to her, stared silently at the others. Belle broke the ice and moaned "WHAT, WHY ON EARTH DON'T I GET A BOW?"

"Calm down, darling, a woman must never shout. Those who shout are not a proper lady. Why, we have a new bell … Who are you my dear?" Bessie asked curiously.

"Boo. My name is Boo," she squeaked.

Finally Benny woke up from his nap, which was more like hibernation! His eyes were glued-to, and he blushed.

"What's up Boo? My name's Billy and this is Belfry" said Billy.

"Billy darling leave the poor girl alone" replied Bessie. Belle, who was being pampered by the cleaner, kept glancing over at Boo and her bow. Bob thought that Boo needs to come out of her shell, so he made a plan. Bessie nodded.

Half an hour later, a wedding was taking place at the church, and all the bells had to ring. There was a jingle from Billy, a low ring from Bob, a deep ring from Benny, Bessie did a loud ring, Belle did a long one, and Boo did a squeak. All of the other bells stared at her. The next day the bells entered a competition on who could ring the loudest. Billy thought that maybe the competition could help Boo. So people arrived in the chilly church and gathered around to hear. Boo huffed and puffed and rang the loudest. Everyone cheered.

Boo just smiled.

When Benny first said 'I love you' to Boo

By Chloe

It all started the day when these five bells, Bessie, Belle, Billy, Bob and Benny rang their bells separately when they should be ringing their sweet melodies together.

"What's happening?" yelled Billy.

"I don't know, but keep still. I'm trying to admire my beautiful self in your not-so-shiny bell," said Belle.

As the two bells kept arguing about who was better than who, ropes and ladders were put all around them. The bell-ringers were climbing up to the bells' dark and damp habitat with a new …

"OMG, that is the shiniest bell I've ever seen, but of course not as shiny as me. She will be perfect for me to see my beautiful face in!" screeched Belle.

A few hours had passed and the new bell had finally been hung up next to Benny.

"Greetings, my name is Bessie, but you can call me Maam or Your Highness. This is Belle."

"Hi, could you keep still so I can look at myself in your shiny glow?"

"Billy."

"Hey, what's up?" said Billy.

"Bob."

"Hello young lady."

"And Benny."

"WOW … ah… err… sorry… hi" said Benny.

"So what brings you here anyway, and what's your name?" said Billy with his pet bat, Belfry.

"Umm … well, my name is Boo and I was put up here to try and help you with your melody, so let's get started I guess!"

Boo started to teach them her old melody that her parents had taught her when she was a baby. There were going off nearly all night. IT DROVE THE NEIGHBOURS CRAZY!! When morning came, the five bells had actually worked together for one, and it actually sounded beautiful.

"Wow, you really made me more confident, Boo. Thanks," murmured Benny. "Yeah, you should chime with us," said Bob excitedly.

"Oh … err… no thanks," said Boo. "But you're amazing," screeched Benny. "OK, I'll try," said Boo.

All six bells chimed their beautiful melody as one big team. It sounded so nice that it drew the whole neighbourhood's attention. It's always better to work as a team.

"I love you Boo!" Benny whispered. Boo whispered back "I love you too!"

And they all lived happily ever after, chiming their captivating melodies across Ruskington.

When Billy scared off the man with the crooked nose

By Enitan

One bright morning, as the dazzling sun was shining through all the weed-filled cracks, it awoke the golden bells. Billy awoke first, because of course he had to feed his small, black pet bat. Belle awoke next, so no-one could take her precious cleaning space in the line. Then came Bessie, Bob, Benny and Boo. This morning something peculiar happened.

A tall, slender man came in the dimly lit room. He looked up at the shining bells. His nose was long and crooked. His eyes were big and wide. And last of all his mouth, a cruel thin mouth. Billy felt a bit cheeky, so he rang his bell as fast and as loud as he possibly could.

The scared man looked around the huge room but no-one was there. He quickly turned around and ran as fast as lightening. He was heading for the big brown door. Once he had gone all the joyful bells cheered happily. No-one was ever going to disturb them again.

When Boo and Belle had a painful adventure

By Lottier

"Hello. I am Boo Bell and I love to hang in the church and sleep!" But one day a burglar took Boo bell and threw her into the forest and she landed in a bush of nettles. "Ouch, that stings," said Boo bell.

Then the burglar took Belle Bell and threw her into the forest where she landed in a tree. "Ouch, that hurts."

Then Boo saw Belle and jumped out of the bush of nettles and went over to the tree that Belle was in and Belle heard Boo's bell and jumped out of the tree and they both saw each other and ran back to the church.

A lady from the church saw Boo and Belle were missing and then she saw them both and put them back in the church. "No more adventures for today!"

When things don't always work out

By Chantelle

Once there were two bells. One of them was called Boo and the other was called Bob. Bob was the old one. Boo was the shiny one. She was the one who doesn't like to ring her bell because she is shy.

Bob read her a little book and Boo got her confidence to ring her bell. It was amazing, and she rang her bell for ever. She got told off and she was sadder than ever that she never rang her bell.

When Bessie stopped being lonely

By Jay

One gloomy morning, when the world was dull and the sun didn't shine, a decision was made; they were to put a bell in All Saints Church. They named the bell Bessie, but Bessie wasn't any plain old bronze bell, she was pure gold with a diamond clapper. At 8:00am, the second Bessie started ringing, the sun appeared out of nowhere!

The sun made everything and everyone too hot so they all stayed indoors with fans. However, Bessie was just lonely and sad to hear about people staying indoors so she prayed to God for a friend. Someone who could make things better. The next thing she knew workers came in the room with a new bell called Belle. Bessie was over the moon.

Belle seemed to be slightly jealous of Bessie because of how unique she was, but Belle could see her reflection so she was happy. When Belle rang clouds appeared and people started coming outside, everyone was happy ..... until it started raining!

Together they prayed for a new member of the belfry, and in the workmen came with a brand new bell called Boo and off they went but ..... more came – Billy, Bob and Benny.

At midnight they all rang together and the world was perfectly balanced.

When Benny asked Boo to marry him

By Ceira

Benny secretly loved Boo so one day he asked Bob for permission to marry her.

So, Benny went and proposed to Boo.

They started to plan their wedding but the church was getting knocked down.

When the church got knocked down they moved churches to Leasingham.

But they find their way to the new church of Ruskington

Then Benny and Boo get married.

Then they go to lovely Hawaii on their honeymoon.

When Benny ran way

By Jersey

On a Sunday morning do you ever wonder what bells do when they are not ringing? Do you just think they are boring old bells made of metal? Well, they are much more than that.

In the belfry, the morning ringing sounded for miles.

Ding! Dong! Ding! Dong!

As usual, Billy was messing up the tune by donging when he should have been dinging. He was such a rascal! The five bells, Belle, Bessie, Boo, Billy and Bob were all trembling with excitement. The big day had finally arrived. At last the tubby bell was in place on his string, but an evil laugh spoiled their greeting to Benny, the new bell. Turning around slowly and shyly, Boo glared at Billy as Benny started to sob with poignancy.

"Are you OK now, Benny?" Boo asked suddenly. Every bell stared at Boo. She had never made such an out-front speech before in front of them all! Benny gaped at her affectionately. "I'm all right, Boo, but thank you for asking!"

"You two would make a good pair. Both goody-two-shoes!" shouted Billy meaningfully. "Stop being so mean, Billy," said Bob. "Anyway it's time to sleep; we've got a wedding tomorrow!"

That night there was a lot of clanging and when Bessie and Boo woke, full of tiredness, Benny was gone! He had obviously run away from that mean, horrible and spiteful Billy.

"I'll go and look for him. Don't worry, Boo, he'll be fine, I promise," said Bessie. And with that she disappeared outside the belfry to find Benny. After a couple of minutes, the sound of bells was heard coming up the stairs, and Benny appeared with Bessie, all tear stained. "I've been so worried, Benny; where have you been and why did you run away?" asked Boo.

"I was in the rose garden. Billy made me so upset that I ran away," exclaimed Benny. "But we'll set things right, don't worry, Benny," said Bessie.

So, in the morning, Bessie, Benny and Boo set things right with Billy and he apologised. So now the wedding was wonderful and the tune rang out, apart from Billy, who did the wrong tune as usual!

When Belle and Bessie got kidnapped

By Ellie

It was a cold winter Friday night and the bells were rehearsing for Saturday and Sunday mornings. Belle and Bessie were glamourising themselves in the mirror. Boo, Bob, Billy and Benny huddled together and talked about how much Bessie and Belle only talk about themselves and their beauty. Bessie was practising for a role as Queen Elizabeth I. Belle was trying to see her reflection in one of the bells' surface and pretending to be on a runway.

Then whilst Bessie and Belle were in the corner, some people walked in and used an axe to cut their ropes and stole them. In a blink of an eye, before Billy could turn around, they were gone. In the church Boo realised that there was no ringing sound.

Boo turned round and shouted "Bessie and Belle are gone!" Even though Boo was she had shouted at the top of her lungs. Billy, Bob and Benny all turned around and saw they had been kidnapped.

The bells all looked and saw the kidnappers driving an Audi A1 and heading to Ruskington Village Hall. The bell-ringers chased after them and caught up with them. They stopped at the village hall. A bell-ringer went inside and found Belle and Bessie being tied to a pole. A kidnapper said, mysteriously, "You have to choose one to go back!". They chose Belle to go home with them, but whispered to Bessie, "We will come and get you at night!"

So that dark, cold winter night the bells left the bell tower to save Bessie. The bell-ringers snuck in quietly and cut the rope and took Bessie back to the bell tower.

On Saturday morning the bells all rang together in a lovely sounding tune of a bell. Bob and all the bells were happy that they got Belle and Bessie back, and so were the bell-ringers. On Sunday everyone woke up in the village and were happy and cheerful. Belfry (Billy's bat) was kept in his cage and slept in!

When Boo broke

By Mathew

There was a church and there were six bells and they were called Boo, Bob, Bessie, Benny, Billy and Belle.

Boo liked to hang on to the window and suddenly the church shook and a part of the building shook so much it might fall and Benny was secretly in love with Boo.

Bob was falling to the ground and then Benny was going after her because they were in love.

Suddenly a parson came into the Church and picked up Boo.

Boo was just hanging on to the roof by herself because they stole the bell.

Boo fell down when the other bells came and she broke and they were all crying.

When Boo's Three Wishes made everyone better

By Erin

One day all the bells were very sick, all of them except little Boo. She wanted to help them. She would have to go on a big stretcher.

They were all wearing their get-well-soon pirate bandanas. (Boo really wanted to wear her bandana.) Bravely she sets out.

After Boo had stepped out of the door she wished she never had and then something made her jump!

She saw that down below her was a lamp. She picked it up and rubbed it and out popped a little genie.

The genie said "Boo, you have three wishes. Tell me what you want and I will grant it. Boo was shocked.

The genie gave her the special medicine for the bells. At that exact moment they all turned and Boo gave them medicine and they all lived happily ever after.

When Belle became famous at the Palace

By Tyla

Belle was a very boasty bell, and loved to show off herself. It was a very exciting day ahead of her but she was losing all her confidence. Billy, Benny and Boo were also worrying very much, but tried not to show it. Bob was on holiday in Buckingham Palace so he couldn't make it to the Queen of Bells' 50th birthday ceremony. The Queen of Bells' name was Bessie, but she made people call her "Your Majesty".

At 2:00pm exactly every one of them rang for the ceremony to start, even Billy didn't make a mistake on purpose. Suddenly the doors swung open and the Queen of Bells walked in.

"Oh, what a lovely sound from the gold bell in the middle. What's their name?"

"Belle," Belle murmured. "Well you obviously love to sing and maybe dance. Would you like to become a famous singer and dancer in my new concert?" "Yes, Queen of Bells, yes!" Belle cried, and she jumped up off her string and landed in front of Bessie and Bessie said, "Gymnast too. I like it!"

On the first day of the concert - it was in Chicago, Belle's home city – Belle was very, very happy about it and even happier she had been chosen out of three other bells – a purple bell (Boo), and blue bell (Benny), and an orange bell called Billy. She was very surprised that she was chosen because she was the ugliest out of every bell in the universe.

She went over to Bessie and mumbled "Why did you pick me? I'm very ugly and vain, so why?" "Because it's not what you show on the outside, it's what shows on the inside, my dearey," answered Bessie.

"Thank you, Your Majesty!"

"Call me Bessie, Bessie Bell!"

When Boo met her best friend

By Nathan

It was eight o'clock on a bright and delightful day when the bells were eating their breakfast. Belle had noticed that Boo wasn't there. She floated upstairs to Boo's bed, but Boo wasn't there. Belle went back downstairs, talked to the others, left a notice on the table and they began their mysterious search.

They hadn't noticed that Boo was floating over the table. She fluttered down to read the notice. The notice said "Meet us at the main ringing area at twelve o'clock. Yours sincerely, the Bells."

When she had read this notice she went into a worried panic. She rushed upstairs under the bed and waited until twelve o'clock.

It was nearly time. Boo rushed to the ringing spot where the others were waiting. They started ringing but when Boo was about to play her not her rope snapped and she fell to the ground.

When she woke up she found herself unharmed. A human had caught her. She started getting scared until she remembered a time when she met this girl.

It was not long until they made friends and the two friends walked off home and they stayed friends for ever.

And that was the story about how Boo's greatest fear became her best friend.

When it's great to be friends together

By Matthew

In the south of Lincolnshire, where faces are always smiling and the sun is always shining, there is a village called Ruskington. This is where our story starts – on a normal Sunday morning.

Twinkling in the aquamarine sky, the sun shone proudly through a vibrant stained-glass window in All Saints Church, making the six golden bells shine proudly in the bell tower.

In the old, dusty bell tower, Billy, who was very naughty and cheeky, was playing with his pet bat, Belfry. Meanwhile Bessie (who thought she was the queen), Boo, Belle and Bob were chatting about their latest performance, having not included Benny because he was not their friend. In the corner Benny, who was often taunted and called "Big Benny", was dreaming about getting married to Boo.

Stealthily Billy crept off with Belfry to the large clock tower (as he was bored of the others talking about their performances) to see the time and play. As he opened the door, Belfry, the bat, flew up high near the clock squeaking loudly in excitement; Billy had gone to save Belfry from getting stuck in the clock and he was now stuck! There was a huge sign of a big regret. At the exact same time Belle danced her way into the bathroom and smashed into the ancient, dusty cream-coloured wall (with a great big SMASH!).

"HHHHEEELLLLP!" they both screamed at the top of their lungs. Trying to solve the problems that had just occurred, Bob explained it couldn't be him going to save them because he was too old. Bessie claimed she was the queen (even though she isn't). Then there was thick silence. It was broken by Boo.

"You can do it!" whispered Boo. "If you help," he replied hopefully.

After a minute or two they decided who was saving who. Benny went up the creaky stairs to the clock. He stepped inside the colossal clock and as the seconds passed Billy turned in the clock at the same speed as the second hand. He started off by de-tangling the trickster's clapper, which was extremely easy, and then he had to de-tangle Billy from the small gap. After a minute of trying, he eventually pulled him out (denting the clock a little bit)! Downstairs, near the store-room, Boo was looking for a new clapper, as Belle had broken the shiny one she owned. It was bad news at the moment, because there were mainly disused or disregarded bells. Suddenly she found one (a little small); she already had tape with her so she taped the clapper to Belle.

Gradually over the next few months Benny and Boo became very good friends (they joked about how they would save the world) and they soon fell madly in love, now that they were heroes as well. Benny was now known as Brave Benny and he had grown a whole four inches in the few months and nobody taunted him – well most of the time. Also, Boo was no longer shy and agreed to ring on their wedding day!

Two months later, on Benny and Boo's wedding day, everyone from the beautiful village was there, and the bells were all wearing a black dress of a black suit with a red rose. There was loads of food and drink; there was an amazing chocolate fountain with glistening strawberries shining brightly. There was loads of confetti waiting to be blasted out of a machine. A few seconds after they kissed confetti came pouring out of the machines and the lovebirds' smile on their faces was as big as an elephant.

As for life, Bessie knew she wasn't the Queen, and Belle found out she wasn't beautiful. Billy was well behaved, well most of the time. Hence Boo and her husband, Benny moved into a private church. Boo and Benny met the other bells three times a year. All the other bells were great friends and tried as hard as they could not to fall out again.

When Billy fell down a hole

By Lucas

One summer day, the bells of Ruskington All Saints Church were having a casual chat in the bell tower, which they did most days. The trees softly swayed in the warm summer breeze and the clock struck twelve o'clock; the bells suddenly started ringing out a lovely tune throughout the village. There were normally always six bells, but today something was different; however, only Boo and Benny realised that one of them, Billy, was missing.

Just to impress Boo, Benny (who had a huge crush on Boo) proudly said that he would go to find the clumsy bell! Benny stepped slowly and cautiously down each and every step of the bell tower, making sure he wouldn't slip. As his shiny yellow feet were tickled by the prickly, swaying grass outside, Benny heard a terrifying scream. He immediately sprinted towards the woods (the direction of the scream). He arrived at the entrance of the woods and starting taking bigger and bigger steps whilst the blinding sun was pounding on him. Because it was so hot, he started to speed up his pace. After a few minutes of running he found a great hole in the ground.

"Is it a cave?" he wondered to himself. Benny then realised it was, in fact, the entrance to an immense cavern.

Benny stepped into the hole. He stood and looked around him; in the distance he heard a kind of crying noise. Benny silently followed the noise until he could see a shimmer of gold. He crept towards the golden flash until he could make out that it was Billy. Benny rushed towards him and Billy looked up to the sound of footsteps. He was so relieved to see Benny; Billy started crying even more. Benny asked Billy if he was alright. Billy nodded slowly and Benny grabbed him by the arm and headed towards the exit.

After several minutes of walking, they gradually made it to the exit. Benny boosted Billy up the hole and Billy pulled Benny up by the hand. Both of the bells made it out of the hole and started to head towards the church.

They eventually both made it back to the church safely and to their home in the bell tower and headed inside. After making it up the stairs everyone was waiting for them at the top of the bell tower.

Benny asked how Billy managed to fall down the hole and Billy explained that he was playing tag with Belfry and wasn't watching where he was going. Just as Belfry was going to tag him he slipped and had tumbled down the hole.

Boo realised that Billy had a massive bruise on his hip, but despite all of that the bells were very proud of what Benny did so they threw a party in celebration for the rescue of the lost bell. At the end of the party Boo managed to save a dance for Benny.

When Benny tempted Belfry down from a tree with dog food

By Jack

In a small, pretty village where everyone is always happy (even the flies are happy) and the trees grow over fifty feet tall, Benny the bell lives. Benny has three not-so-good friends – Billy, Belle and Bessie; his best friends are Boo and Bob.

It was a lovely winter's morning when suddenly Billy's pet bat, Belfry, flew as quick as a flash, hot out of the window and with amazing speed went outside. It was heart-breaking for Billy (he thought he'd lost his friend forever), but he still followed him. Bob shouted as loud as he can "No, Billy, stay in here". But Billy ran after his bat.

Billy ran swiftly through the old, wet, scary wood. Boo – who is always shy - ran carelessly with Benny after Billy, but Billy was too fast. The wood had the tallest trees and no flowers around. All there was were mushrooms and bugs, so many little spiders, cockroaches, wood lice and rats – so, so, so many rats it was horrible.

At that very moment, they saw a shimmer of light from Billy's bronze coat. It blinded them for that moment and when they opened their eyes they saw Billy. Billy was climbing a tree – he was still climbing. Bessie would not climb the tree because she has the biggest fear of birds. Belle just hates her make-up getting smudged. Boo hates the feeling of being on top of the highest tree in the whole woods.

Benny yelled "Come down now; I'm sure Belfry will come down."

But Billy yelled right back at him, "No, I'm too high, I'm going to fall, and I'm scared!"

So, all the bells came up with a plan to get Billy and Belfry down.

Surprisingly, it was Benny going up the tree. Everyone gulped, even Benny gulped, but Bob had the littlest bit of hope and that gave Benny a massive boost so climbed that tree and got Billy down and Bob got Belfry down with a bit of dog food. Benny asked if he could have a small conversation with Boo and with all his happiness he asked Boo to go out with him. But at first Boo couldn't decide, but eventually she blushed and replied, "Yes!"

And all the bells lived an amazing life. Billy never went outside without the other bells, Benny was now called a hero and life in the church was better. It was not boring; it was fun for Billy and every day they went out and everyone was good and Bob, after years of being miserable, was eventually happy.

When poorly Bob got a boost

By Luke

One scorching hot summer day, the ecstatic, shiny bells in the brick belfry swung joyfully. They were playing happily while the sun beat down heavily on the small church. Nobody was in the church so they could chime as much as they wanted.

It seemed like a normal day; but it wasn't. Unusually Bob wasn't telling one of his annoyingly boring stories. Boo was the first to notice.

"Guys," she whispered. No-one was listening. Stepping out of her comfort zone, she screamed at the top of her lungs "GUYS! Bob's not well!"

Everyone stopped, open-mouthed in shock. Silence filled the tower. Boo blushed intensely. The atmosphere faded quickly as they realised that she was right. Something was wrong with Bob. Later that night ……. "So here's the plan," Benny whispered to Boo. "You're going to raise money for Bob to get better by staying as still as possible for as long as possible …."

"But what are you going to do?" enquired Boo. Benny grinned – a look of delight on his face. "I'm going to enter a sandwich-eating tournament! Yummy, yummy in my tummy, I'll be sure to win first place!"

The next day Benny missed his breakfast, brunch and lunch, as well as all the snacks he usually had in between! He was so ravenous he couldn't even think straight. Casually he left the old, damp church on his was to the contest with a rumbling tummy.

Meanwhile Boo was preparing herself to be as calm and silent as possible. She needed to raise as much money as she could.

At the same time Bessie was in London having tea with the Queen. She had heard what was said the night before and decided to take matters into her own hands. She sipped her warm drink and asked politely,

"Please can I borrow some money?" "Why do you want *my* money, may I ask?" queried the Queen. "Well, my friend Bob is very ill and we need a lot of money to re-furnish him. My other friends are being sponsored for different challenges, but I don't think it will be enough."

"Of course!" exclaimed Her Majesty, "But I want to be able to make a grand entrance before giving you the money. I want to be able to wear my most luxurious robes and crown and I want to be able to hold you to an oath that says that you owe me a favour."

"OK, you can have all that as long as you help my friend get better - deal or no deal?" Bessie said, holding out her hand to shake the Queen's. "Deal!"

In the centre of Ruskington a crowd gathered. "Benny! Benny! Benny! Benny!" chanted the masses as Benny ate his fiftieth sandwich of the minute. His opponent – who was about to give up – sat with defeat in his eyes. Aaaaaand ….. "Yes!" yelled Benny, a look of pure delight on his face.

Close by Boo was taking a break. She was counting her coins when Benny sprinted over and announced that he had won £20,000 from the competition. He told her that she didn't need any more money. "That's great!" exclaimed Boo. "I know!" Benny replied. Unable to contain their exhilaration the pair entered their home to find something extremely bizarre. Belle – who disliked everything except herself, fashion and make-up – was on a laptop. She wore a worried expression.

"Um guys, how much money did you get?" Benny looked at Boo. "I've got £50," she said nervously. "That gives us a total of £20,050." "That's not enough," Belle said.

Slowly the old oak door with a rusty, metal look creaked open and all heads were turned. Bessie strolled in with Her Majesty the Queen striding beside her. She was wearing her finest robes made from the best silk anyone could ask for.

"Whoa!" everyone said in unison.

"How much do you need?" the Queen asked.

Boo, who was hyper-ventilating, stared blankly.

"£9,000," Belle said quickly, stepping in for Boo.

"Really? I thought it would be more than that."

Realising just how much money the Queen had, Belle blinked and smiled. Handing a cheque to Benny, she said "Toodle ooh," and walked out of the church hurriedly. Bessie remained.

"How did you get the Queen of England, Queen Elizabeth, to come to our church and hand over money?" Boo questioned in a quiet vvoice. "I just went to Buckingham Palace, and tea with her and told her about Bob being ill. It was simple really." Bessie shrugged as if it wasn't a big deal. "Anyway, we need to help Bob. We have the money now, don't we?" Turning to Belle she ordered her to ring the bell fixing service. "Say that we need them urgently!"

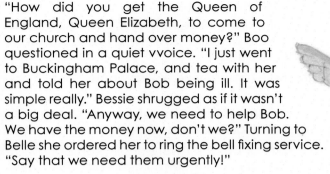

A few hours later, two men entered the building and took a look at Bob. "He's quite battered and bruised, but he will live to see another day," one of the men explained to Belle.

"What sort of price are we looking at?" wondered Boo. She had been standing awkwardly in one corner of the room but she decided to make herself seen. The man turned towards her.

"About £15,000 I would say," the man stated in a matter-of-fact way. "OK, we can pay that," Boo replied. "In fact, we can pay you the money right now if we wanted to." "Then why don't you?" dared the man. The words were softly spoken, but it was still a direct challenge.

"OK!" She turned around. "Billy, please can you come here and give the man some money." "How much?" Billy asked, taking a wad of cash out of his pocket. "£15,000," Boo told him.

They made the exchange and the men left the building. When everyone looked at Bob nobody recognised him. He was a good as new.

"Wow!" Everyone was stunned. Even Bessie had to admit that he looked great and a flicker of disbelief flashed across her face.

The next day ...... Everyone was playing again, swinging around the belfry. Belfry the bat fluttered around aimlessly. Everything was back to normal..

The campaign to restore the six bells of Ruskington village to their full glory

The sound of Parish Church bells has been part of Ruskington life for over 400 years. The peel of six bells located in the bell tower of All Saints Parish Church date back to 1593* when two bells were installed, followed in 1882 by two more and finally another two in 1911.

In 2014, the 422-year-old tenor bell became unsafe to ring – remedial work was carried out at the time.

On investigation, it was also discovered that 1911 was also the last time the bells were re-hung and any real investment made into 'keeping them safe and sound for the future'.

Action was needed: the bells were still just about safe to ring, but they were ringing on borrowed time. So, a team of Ruskington locals came together in January 2016 to formulate a plan to involve the whole village and its businesses to raise a required £50,000. So, two Parties in the Car Park (thanks to the Shoulder of Mouton), a couple of Christmas fairs, sponsored bike rides, taking part in the BBC's Music Day, several coffee mornings and afternoon teas later... the figure of £50,000 was in sight.

At the time of writing, the project team's aim is to have the bells booked in for their face-lift before 2020.

Please continue to visit our Facebook page – Ruskington Bells – for how we are coming along. Thank you to everyone! Hurrah!!

Any questions or donations, contact us at: <u>bellsruskington@gmail.com</u>

Listen to a recording of the bells in full flight on YouTube – just search under *Ruskington Bells*.

Printed in the United States
By Bookmasters